mortimer's first garden

In memory of Bob Bruzas, an avid gardener
who planted love and Sonshine—K. W.

For Kaitlin Farnsworth—D. A.

MARGARET K. McELDERRY BOOKS

An imprint of Simon & Schuster Children's Publishing Division

1230 Avenue of the Americas, New York, New York 10020

Text copyright © 2009 by Karma Wilson

Illustrations copyright © 2009 by Dan Andreasen

All rights reserved, including the right of reproduction in whole or in part in any form.

Book design by Debra Sfetsios and Sonia Chaghatzbanian

The text for this book is set in Bell MT.

The illustrations for this book are rendered in oil on bristol board.

Manufactured in China

10 9 8 7 6 5 4 3 2 1

Library of Congress Cataloging-in-Publication Data

Wilson, Karma.

Mortimer's first garden / Karma Wilson; illustrated by Dan Andreasen.—1st ed. p. cm.

Summary: Little Mortimer Mouse, longing to see something green at winter's end, follows the lead of
the big people and plants, waters, and weeds his last sunflower seed until, finally, with God's help and a
lot of patience, he harvests his crop.

ISBN-13: 978-1-4169-4203-0

ISBN-10: 1-4169-4203-3

[1. Gardening—Fiction. 2. Mice—Fiction.] I. Andreasen, Dan, ill. II. Title. PZ7.W69656Mof 2009

[E]—dc22

2007037802

mortimer's
first
garden

by karma wilson
illustrated by dan andreasen

MARGARET K. McELDERRY BOOKS
New York London Toronto Sydney

Little Mortimer Mouse
looked outside. "Brown, brown, brown,"
he squeaked. "Nothing but brown! Too
dull, too drab, too dreary!"

Mortimer longed to see something
green. Anything green.

"Well, at least I have these!" He
nibbled the shell off one of three
sunflower seeds he had saved.
"Nothing is as good as sunflower
seeds," he said.

Just then the big people
came into the room.
One of them said,
*"Children, it's springtime.
What time is that?"*

"Garden time!" shouted
the children.

Munch, munch, munch.
Mortimer nibbled his treat.

"What's a garden?"
he wondered.

Mortimer perked up his ears. "Seeds?" he squeaked.
Anything about seeds could be tasty.

Mortimer nibbled the shell off his second seed.

Munch, munch, munch. Delicious!

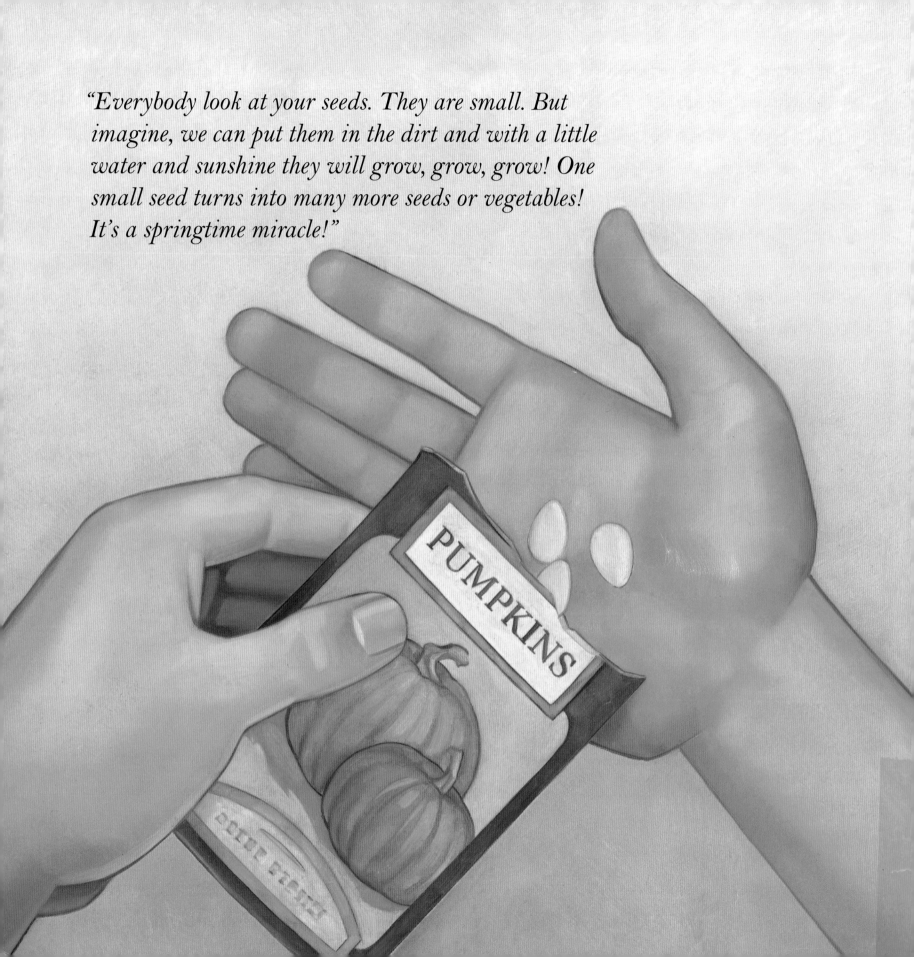

"Everybody look at your seeds. They are small. But imagine, we can put them in the dirt and with a little water and sunshine they will grow, grow, grow! One small seed turns into many more seeds or vegetables! It's a springtime miracle!"

Mortimer giggled at the thought. "I don't believe a word of it! Seeds are for eating. Who would throw perfectly good food in the dirt?"

He picked up his last seed and looked at it. "But what if the miracle is true?" Mortimer wondered. "Can one little seed turn into many?"

"Let's go plant seeds, and soon everything will be green!"

"Green?" thought Mortimer. That settled it. "I will plant my sunflower seed!" he said.

Mortimer searched and searched for the right place.
"I need somewhere the sun will shine. And somewhere
I can get water." Then Mortimer saw it.

The perfect spot.

Mortimer dug and dug and dug.

He held up his precious seed. It looked delicious.
But Mortimer dropped the seed into the dirt anyway.

"I hope the miracle comes true," he said, patting soil carefully around
the seed. Then he found an acorn cap and lugged over capfuls of water
from a small puddle of melted snow.

"Phew. Gardening is hard work!"

Mortimer looked at his garden. Nothing but brown dirt. He looked up.
The sky was gray.

"We'll see," he said.

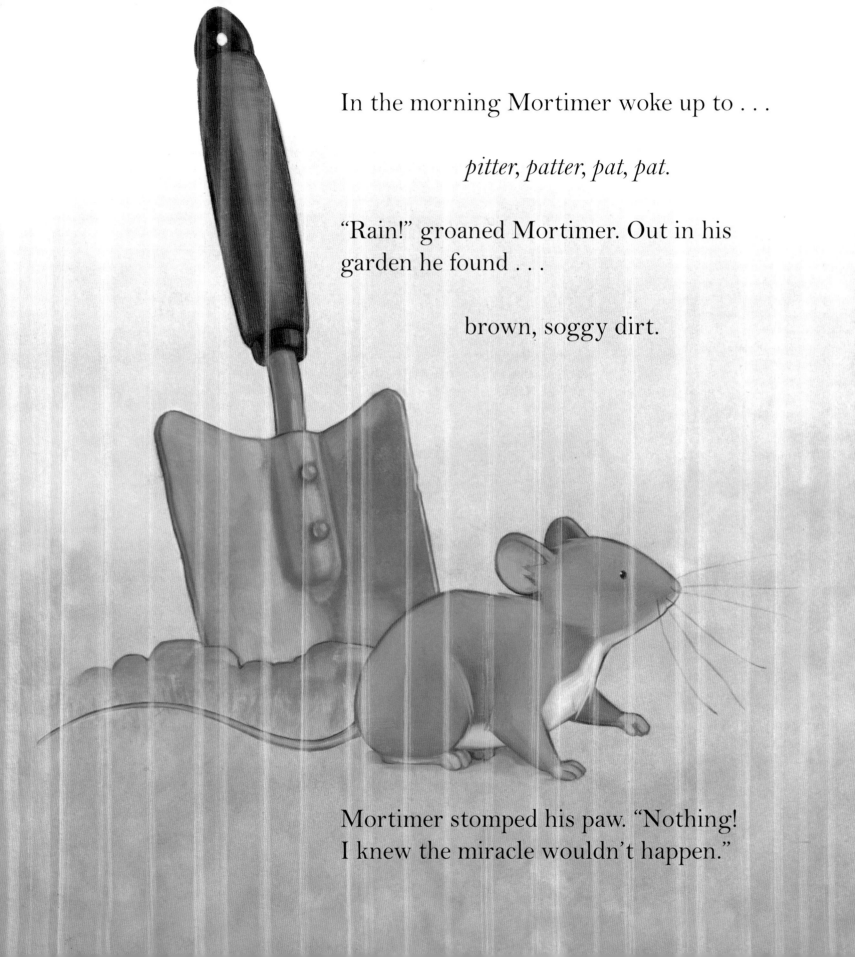

In the morning Mortimer woke up to . . .

pitter, patter, pat, pat.

"Rain!" groaned Mortimer. Out in his garden he found . . .

brown, soggy dirt.

Mortimer stomped his paw. "Nothing! I knew the miracle wouldn't happen."

"I'm going to dig my seed back up and eat it!"
Mortimer said. But then he stopped. "Maybe
some miracles need more time."

He looked up at the sky, and down to his seed.
"Please grow and turn green," he said.

The next morning Mortimer
woke up to . . .

pitter, patter, pat, pat.

"Oh, no. Rain again!" he said.

Outside Mortimer found . . .

brown, soggy dirt!

"No, no, no!" squeaked Mortimer.
"This won't do! My seed will never
grow. How much time do miracles take
anyway?" cried Mortimer. "If I don't
dig up my seed now, it might rot in all
this rain."

But a gentle, quiet voice said, *"Wait."*

"Who was that?" whispered Mortimer.

"Wait," said the voice again. Only it wasn't just a voice. It was a feeling in Mortimer's heart.

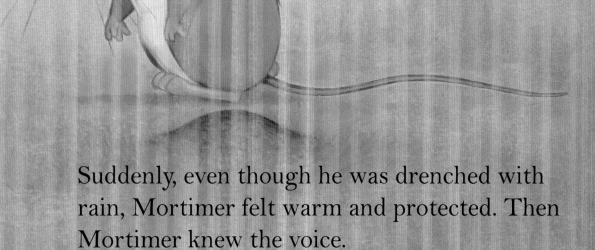

Suddenly, even though he was drenched with rain, Mortimer felt warm and protected. Then Mortimer knew the voice.

Mortimer bowed his head. "I will wait, God. But please, make my seed grow."

And Mortimer waited.

On the third morning Mortimer
woke to a light in his eyes. Sunshine!
Bold and bright and beautiful!

Mortimer scampered outside and found . . .

GREEN!

Where his seed had been buried, two tiny green leaves poked up through the earth.

Mortimer danced and Mortimer pranced. He skipped around and around the tiny plant.

"My garden!" he cried. "My miracle! Thank you, God!"

Then he stopped. His plant was so small. And what was that next to it?
A weed! Mortimer plucked the weed and watered the baby plant.

And every day after,
Mortimer checked his garden.

He weeded, he watered,
and he waited . . .

and waited . . .

and waited. . . .

And in the summer warmth
the tiny seed continued to grow . . .

and grow . . .

and grow. . . .

Until one day in his garden Mortimer found . . .

YELLOW!

A giant sunflower had bloomed. Bold and bright and beautiful, just like the sun.

Up, up, up climbed Mortimer. Down, down, down he looked. Mortimer felt as if he could see forever!

"My sunflower!" cried Mortimer. "It *is* a miracle! Thank you, God!"

Soon the sunflower
was heavy with seeds.

"Hundreds of seeds," squeaked Mortimer. "All from just one. I've never seen such a wonder!" He plucked each of the seeds and lugged them home to store away.

That night Mortimer cozied down into a bed of seeds and smiled. He stretched and yawned.

"Thank you, God, for my first garden," Mortimer said, looking at his bountiful pile.

There were plenty of seeds to eat, plenty of seeds to plant next spring, and even a few to share. "And please, God," Mortimer prayed, "I wouldn't mind a friend to help me eat these."

And Mortimer fell fast asleep.